Ally Protects the La Jolla Seals

Written by **Deborah Saracini**

Illustrated by **Neethi Joseph (Folks Fables)**

Published by Miriam Laundry Publishing Company
miriamlaundry.com

PB ISBN 978-1-990107-34-4
e-Book ISBN 978-1-990107-35-1

Printed in USA   FIRST EDITION

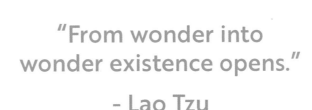

"From wonder into
wonder existence opens."

- Lao Tzu

To Rama, who taught me to have
a reverence for life.

Thank you to the Sierra Club Seal Society and
the La Jolla Friends of the Seals docents, the
Seal Conservancy and Animal Protection &
Rescue League for all your heartfelt dedication
in protecting and educating the public about
the La Jolla Seals and Sea Lions.

Love and gratitude to my dear friends —
Nancy, Kathy, Lea, Barb, Elizabeth and Lisa,
to my sister — De, my brother — Dan, and
my wonderful cousin — Brian, for all your
encouragement and creative ideas.

And to my niece, Ally ... You are my inspiration.
I am so proud of everything you do!

Ally was snorkeling in La Jolla when she felt something tug on her flippers.

"Eeeek!" she screamed.

She twisted around and saw a brown spotted seal pup. He tugged on her flippers again, swam off and came back to tug once more.

He's playing with me, Ally realized. *He's playing with me just like my puppy, Benji, does!*

And as she surfaced to swim to shore, the pup swam right up to her face and touched noses with her!

As she walked out of the water, laughing, she saw lots of people surrounding a group of seals. They were taking selfies, touching the seals and kicking sand on them. Frightened, the mother seals scooted on their bellies back into the ocean, leaving their pups alone and crying.

6

Ally ran over to the crowd. "Stop! Please stand back from the seals!" she pleaded. "You're scaring them!"

But the crowds didn't listen to her. They laughed, shouted, and moved in closer.

What can I do? No one is listening to me! And then Ally spotted a few of her friends who quickly came to help her. A nearby lifeguard joined them too. Soon, people were watching the seals from the sidewalk, and the mother seals began returning to their crying pups, bonding by touching noses.

Even though the seals were now resting peacefully on the beach, and the moms had returned to the pups, Ally knew that the seals could be disturbed again as soon as she left.

FUN FACT

Mother seals identify their pups through scent and bond by touching noses.

And then she had an idea ...

"I know what I can do ... I can start a petition drive to close the beach to people when the seals are bonding with their moms! I'll get it signed by all my friends, family, and classmates. Maybe they'll persuade everyone they know, too!"

Ally was so excited and told her mom about her plan on the ride home in the car.

"I'm very proud of you for thinking about this, Ally," her mom said. "You'll need to do some internet research first to learn why the seals need to be protected."

Ally went to her school library and researched the biology and behavior of the seals. She found out that disturbing their natural behavior could have negative effects, especially during the pup-birthing season.

Ally looked up from the computer. "But the birthing season is right now!" she exclaimed.

FUN FACT

The birthing or "pupping" season for the seals in La Jolla is from December 15 to May 15. Most pups are born in the months of February and March.

FUN FACT

In recent years as many as 50 pups are born during the pupping season in La Jolla.

FUN FACT

Pups are born on the beach in La Jolla, and weigh 20-25 pounds at birth.

After Ally explained all this to the crowd of students around her, her friends wanted to help. Jasmine, Alicia, and Lakshmi agreed to spread the word about the petition.

But Joey grumbled, "The seals keep having pups here every year, and I know they're *not* endangered. So, I'm not worried."

Jeffrey also argued, "Besides, I like to use the beach to go swimming, and I have more rights than the seals. They can just go somewhere else."

Oh no, Ally thought as her heart sank. *Looks like there are definitely two opposing sides on this subject.*

At home, her mom asked, "What's wrong, Ally?"

Ally told her mom about Joey and Jeffrey.

"How can they be so selfish, when we all know there are no other beaches without people? We would have to take a boat to see them at an off-shore island!"

"You know, Ally, Aunt Nancy is friends with a Marine Biologist. Maybe she can help you..."

Ellen, the Marine Biologist, gave Ally lots of good information for her petition in favor of closing the beach during pupping season.

"This little beach in La Jolla is called Casa Beach, or Children's Pool, and is a federally recognized rookery. It is bordered by a seawall that keeps sand on the beach year-round for the seals to haul out and provides a great place to view the seals without disturbing them."

Harbor seals "haul out" (come out of the water) to rest, warm up, re-oxygenate, and molt or shed their fur. During pupping season, they use the beach to give birth, nurse, and raise their pups. If pups are not able to rest and nurse on the beach, they won't build up a blubber layer necessary to forage for food in the cold water.

A group of seals is called a "colony", and a place where seals are born is called a "rookery".

Most of the other rookeries are in Northern California, and all of them are protected and closed to prevent human disturbance during the vulnerable pupping season, except this one.

17

Ally took notes as Ellen continued.

"There are lots of other places for people to swim. There's actually seven other beaches in La Jolla, and all are more suitable for swimming than this one, which has dangerous rocky outcrops and rip currents. Also, did you know that people come from all over the world to see the seals in this natural environment?" Ellen asked in amazement.

FUN FACT

Casa Beach is home to 250 seals year-round, and the next closest one is much smaller and 160 miles north.

FUN FACT

Casa Beach is very important to the marine life ecosystem. The seals create a healthy ocean environment for fish. Their waste is eaten by small creatures that fish feed on, keeping the fish stock plentiful, which helps to counterbalance the issues caused by overfishing.

FUN FACT

La Jolla can be translated from Spanish as "the jewel".

"I do," replied Ally. "Some of our out-of-town friends have said they've even seen the seals on the covers the tourist magazines!"

"That's right," Ellen replied enthusiastically. "These seals draw tourist business to the nearby hotels, restaurants, and shops. Many studies have concluded that adults and children would rather have the awe-inspiring education of watching the seals than use this beach to swim."

A light bulb went off in Ally's head when Ellen mentioned the tourist business. She couldn't wait to tell her friends about her plan.

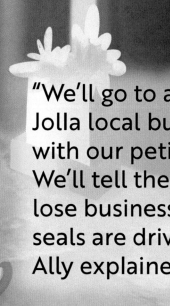

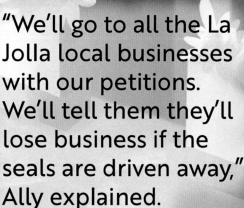

"We'll go to all the La Jolla local businesses with our petitions. We'll tell them they'll lose business if the seals are driven away," Ally explained.

In addition to splitting up to cover the La Jolla businesses, Jasmine had many people sign the petitions at her Hip Hop dance performance ....

Alicia took the petitions to her brother's big Mexican wedding ....

Lakshmi got lots of signatures at her family's Indian restaurant ....

With the help of her friends and classmates, Ally was able to get hundreds of signatures on her petition.

21

But when she showed her mom the petitions that night, her mom asked, "And what are you going to do with them?"

"Well, I'll...I guess I'll..." Ally was confused. "I don't know," she admitted.

"If you're really serious, you will have to present your petitions to the officials at City Council. They have the authority to close the beach," her mom explained.

Ally gulped. "City Council? Me?"

On the day of the presentation, Ally had butterflies in her stomach. *I can't speak in front of the City Council,* she thought when she arrived. *There are so many people here, too!* But then she remembered how important it was for her to speak for the seals, who could not speak for themselves.

When her name was called, Ally walked slowly with the huge stack of petitions and placed them carefully on the table in front of the City Council members.

Ally took a deep breath. "Um ... Good morning," she began hesitantly. "I am here to present my signed petitions and ... and ask for your ... your approval to close Casa Beach in La Jolla during seal pupping season." Ally explained why this was important — to the seals and to local businesses.

"Thank you, Ally," one council member said. "It's wonderful that you've taken on this initiative to save our natural world."

Ally knew that she would have to wait for their decision. She could barely eat and sleep for the next week. And then ...

Ally was thrilled when, on December 15, a chain-link fence was installed across the stairs and a sign was posted.

CITY OF SAN DIEGO
BEACH CLOSED

Soon, the beach was filled with mom-and-pup pairs, bonding by touching noses and nursing.

"Look at the pups riding on their moms' backs!" Jasmine exclaimed, pointing to a few pairs swimming in the sparkling pool.

"Wow, that pup just climbed up on the low rocks after trying and trying!" said Alicia, laughing.

"This is so cool! We can be close and nobody is bothering them!" Lakshmi said with a big smile.

"What a magical place this is. You never know what you can do if you try!" Ally exclaimed to her friends. "This place is truly the jewel of La Jolla!"

GLOSSARY

CITY COUNCIL
City officials who, together with the California Coastal Commission, have the authority to close the beach for the seals' pupping season.

HAULING OUT
When seals leave the water to gain access to the sand, usually for purposes of resting, warming, re-oxygenating, nursing pups, or molting.

MOLT
Annual shedding of skin and hair during warmer months of the year. Harbor seals molt about a month after breeding season over a period of 1 - 2 months.

PINNIPED
Means "fin-footed", and refers to the marine mammals that have front and hind flippers. This includes seals, sea-lions and walruses.

PUPPING SEASON
A 5-month period during which pups are born. Varies with the climate: from February in the southern range (Baja), February and March in Southern California, and June in Alaska.

RE-OXYGENATE

Harbor seals reduce their heart rate when they dive down to 1640 feet, and restore their oxygen supply when they surface.

ROOKERY

Refers to a location regularly used for the breeding and rearing of young pinnipeds.

RIP CURRENT

A narrow but strong current that flows away from the beach.

SITE FIDELITY

Harbor seals have "site fidelity", which means that they stay at the same resting, haul out, and birthing site. They may wander in search of food but will often return to home base.

SEAL MILK

Seal milk is a source of nourishment consisting of approximately 69% fat and 10% protein. It serves to provide adequate nourishment for the pup through the nursing period (4 to 7 weeks) to double the birth weight.

LA JOLLA

About the Author

Deborah Saracini has been a Docent Coordinator and Trainer for the Sierra Club Seal Society and La Jolla Friends of the Seals since 2007. She became interested in the La Jolla seals when she had a personal encounter with a seal pup on her beach. She became both an educator and political activist, working with others to successfully lobby San Diego City Council and the California Coastal Commission to close Casa Beach/Children's Pool for the annual harbor seal pupping season.

Deborah lives in Del Mar, CA, with her Westie and Scottie terriers, her pups of the land. You can contact her at **www.facebook.com/DebSaracini**